THE JACKAL AND THE RATS

ONE DAY, WHILE ROAMING IN THE FOREST IN SEARCH OF FOOD, A JACKAL SUDDENLY SPIED A TROOP OF RATS. THEIR KING WAS A HUGE BANDICOOT.

I COULD ATTACK THEM. BUT THEN I'D CATCH ONLY ONE AND THE REST WOULD RUN AWAY.

IF I'M CLEVER, HOWEVER, THESE RATS COULD PROVIDE ME WITH FOOD FOR MANY DAYS.

SO HE FOLLOWED THEM TO THEIR HOLE.

WHEN THE LAST OF THEM HAD GONE INTO THE HOLE, THE JACKAL STOOD OUTSIDE ON ONE LEG, HIS MOUTH OPEN AND HIS FACE TURNED TOWARDS THE SUN.

1

A LITTLE LATER, WHEN THE RATS CAME OUT AGAIN—

WHY ARE YOU STANDING ON ONE LEG?

IF I STOOD ON ALL FOUR, THE EARTH WOULD NOT BE ABLE TO BEAR MY WEIGHT.

WHY DO YOU KEEP YOUR MOUTH OPEN?

TO TAKE IN AIR, MY ONLY FOOD.

AND WHY IS YOUR FACE TURNED UPWARDS?

TO WORSHIP THE SUN.

HOW LUCKY WE ARE TO HAVE A SAINT IN OUR MIDST! WE SHALL WORSHIP HIM EVERY MORNING AND EVENING.

IT HAS WORKED! HE REALLY THINKS I AM A SAINT!

THE NEXT MORNING—

AH! HERE THEY COME. I MUST POSE AGAIN FOR THEM.

2

SO THAT EVENING AS THE RATS WERE READY TO SET OUT —

TODAY ALL OF YOU GO AHEAD. I'LL COME OUT LAST.

IF MY GUESS IS CORRECT, HE'LL POUNCE ON ME. I MUST BE READY.

THE NEXT MOMENT THE JACKAL SPRANG AT HIM...

... BUT MISSED.

SO THIS IS YOUR GAME! YOU RASCAL!

THE BANDICOOT DUG HIS TEETH INTO THE JACKAL'S THROAT AND KILLED HIM.

BACK CAME ALL THE OTHER RATS AND THEY HAD A GRAND FEAST.

THE JACKAL AND THE LION

A HUNGRY JACKAL ONCE SUDDENLY CAME ACROSS A LION WHO WAS ON HIS WAY HOME.

WHAT DO YOU WANT?

I CANNOT HOPE TO ESCAPE. IT WOULD BE WISER TO PLAY HUMBLE.

MY LORD, PLEASE LET ME BE YOUR HUMBLE SERVANT.

ALL RIGHT.

WHAT LUCK! I'LL NEVER HAVE TO GO HUNGRY AGAIN.

FOLLOW ME.

WHEN THEY REACHED THE LION'S DEN—

YOUR WORD IS MY COMMAND, MY LORD.

IF YOU DO AS I TELL YOU, YOU WILL BE WELL FED.

YOU WILL GO TO THE TOP OF THE MOUNTAIN EACH DAY AND SEE IF THERE ARE ANY ANIMALS ROAMING IN THE VALLEY BELOW.

AND IF I SEE ONE, MY LORD?

YOU WILL COME AND TELL ME ABOUT IT. THEN YOU WILL SAY: "SHINE FORTH IN ALL YOUR MIGHT, MY LORD."

THEN, AFTER I'VE KILLED THE ANIMAL AND EATEN MY FILL, YOU MAY TAKE WHAT'S LEFT.

SO THE NEXT DAY THE JACKAL WENT TO THE MOUNTAIN TOP.

AH! THERE'S AN ELEPHANT!

HE SPED BACK TO THE LION...

...AND FELL AT HIS FEET.

I'VE SEEN AN ELEPHANT. SHINE FORTH IN ALL YOUR MIGHT, MY LORD.

THE LION KILLED THE ELEPHANT...

...AND ATE HIS FILL.

NOW YOU MAY EAT THE REST.

AS THE DAYS WENT BY, THE JACKAL GREW FATTER AND FATTER.

BUT, ALAS! HE GREW LESS AND LESS HUMBLE. ONE DAY—

WHY SHOULD I LIVE ON LEFTOVER FOOD? I, TOO, AM A FOUR-FOOTED CREATURE! WHY WORK FOR THE LION WHEN I COULD KILL ELEPHANTS AND BUFFALOES FOR MYSELF?

AFTER ALL, THE LION ONLY GETS HIS STRENGTH FROM THE MAGIC PHRASE, " GO FORTH AND SHINE IN ALL YOUR MIGHT".

HE APPEALED TO THE LION.

MY LORD, I HAVE LIVED FOR TOO LONG ON WHAT YOU KILL. I WOULD LIKE TO EAT AN ELEPHANT I HAVE KILLED MYSELF.

THE LION WAS SILENT FOR A WHILE.

WHAT A FOOLISH IDEA! HE'LL BE KILLED HIMSELF!

THE JACKAL NIMBLY BOUNDED AWAY...

...ON THE TRAIL OF THE ELEPHANT.

I'LL CATCH HIM BY THE THROAT AND KILL HIM.

HE SPRANG AT THE ELEPHANT...

...BUT MISSED HIM.

THE PUZZLED ELEPHANT JUST WALKED OVER HIM...

...AND THAT WAS THE END OF THE FOOLHARDY JACKAL.

THE CLEVER JACKAL

A GROUP OF ROGUES WERE ONCE HAVING A GRAND PARTY.

TOWARDS MIDNIGHT—

CAN I HAVE SOME MORE MEAT?

YOU CAN HAVE MORE WINE IF YOU LIKE, BUT THERE'S NO MEAT LEFT.

WHAT! NO MEAT! BUT I MUST HAVE SOME!

I'LL GO TO THE CHARNEL-GROVE, KILL A PROWLING JACKAL, AND BRING YOU ITS MEAT.

CLUB IN HAND, THE BRAGGART SWAGGERED OFF.

WHEN HE REACHED THE GROVE —

I'LL PRETEND I'M A CORPSE. THAT WILL ATTRACT JACKALS AND KEEP AWAY LIONS AND TIGERS.

WHEN A JACKAL COMES NEAR, I'LL KILL HIM WITH MY CLUB.

A LITTLE LATER, A PACK OF JACKALS CAME BY.

LOOK, THERE'S A CORPSE. COME ON!

WAIT! LET ME MAKE SURE WE'RE SAFE.

SNIFF! SNIFF!

THE SMELL OF A LIVING MAN! JUST AS I THOUGHT! HE IS ONLY PRETENDING TO BE DEAD.

JUST THEN HE NOTICED THE CLUB.

HE IS PROBABLY WAITING TO KILL ONE OF US.

WAIT HERE. I'LL TAKE CARE OF THE RASCAL.

HE CREPT UP TO THE MAN···

···CAUGHT THE CLUB WITH HIS TEETH···

···AND GAVE IT A SLIGHT TUG.

IT MUST BE A BANDICOOT! I'D BETTER TIGHTEN MY GRIP.

THE NEXT MOMENT THE JACKAL LET GO OF THE CLUB WITH A JERK.

THE STARTLED ROGUE JUMPED TO HIS FEET, FLUNG HIS CLUB AT THE JACKAL · · ·

· · · AND MISSED!

I DARE NOT FACE MY FRIENDS AFTER MY VAIN BOAST.

I'D BETTER GO HOME AND SLEEP.

14

THE JACKAL AND THE MAGIC SPELL

IN A SECLUDED SPOT IN A FOREST, THE FAMILY PRIEST OF BRAHMADATTA, KING OF VARANASI, WAS ONCE REPEATING A SECRET SPELL.

A JACKAL LYING NEAR BY PRICKED UP HIS EARS.

IF I LISTEN CAREFULLY I, TOO, CAN MASTER THAT.

A LITTLE LATER THE BRAHMAN GOT UP.

THERE! I'VE MASTERED IT.

THE NEXT MOMENT, TO HIS SURPRISE, A JACKAL STOOD BEFORE HIM.

HO! BRAHMAN, YOU COULDN'T HAVE MASTERED THE SPELL BETTER THAN I.

AND OFF HE RAN. THE PRIEST RAN AFTER HIM.

I MUST CATCH HIM! HE'LL PLAY HAVOC WITH THAT SPELL.

BUT THE JACKAL ESCAPED DEEP INTO THE FOREST.

I'LL FIRST GET MARRIED AND THEN, USING THE SPELL, I'LL BRING ALL THE FOUR-FOOTED CREATURES OF THE FOREST UNDER MY SWAY.

HE SOON FOUND HIMSELF A SHE-JACKAL.

IF YOU BECOME MY WIFE YOU SHALL BE QUEEN OF ALL THE ANIMALS OF THE FOREST.

I'M WILLING.

SNIFF SNIFF

LATER HE UTTERED THE SPELL AND ALL THE ANIMALS BEGAN TO FLOCK TOWARDS HIM.

YOU ARE OUR MASTER, O MIGHTY ONE!

YOU ARE OUR KING!

THEY SEATED THE JACKAL AND HIS WIFE ON A LION WHICH STOOD ON TWO ELEPHANTS.

THEY CONFERRED A TITLE ON THE JACKAL AND BOWED TO HIM.

HAIL!

HAIL!

HAIL SARVADATA, CHOSEN KING OF THE ANIMALS!

ALL THIS WENT TO THE JACKAL'S HEAD.

MY SUBJECTS, WE SHALL CAPTURE THE CITY OF VARANASI.

SO, WITH HIS GREAT FOLLOWING, HE MARCHED TO VARANASI.

WE SHALL CAMP HERE AND SEND A MESSAGE TO THE KING.

WHEN THE KING RECEIVED THE MESSAGE, HIS FAMILY PRIEST WAS WITH HIM.

"SURRENDER YOUR KINGDOM OR DIE FIGHTING FOR IT," HE SAYS.

HE HAS STRUCK TERROR EVERY-WHERE. HIS CAMP COVERS AN AREA OF THIRTY-SIX MILES! WHO IS THIS ANIMAL?

HE IS SARVADATA, THE JACKAL-KING. LEAVE HIM TO ME. I'LL FIND A WAY OF DEFEATING HIM.

ALL RIGHT. MAY YOU BE SUCCESSFUL.

I MUST FIRST FIND OUT WHAT HE INTENDS TO DO.

O SARVADATA, HOW DO YOU PLAN TO TAKE THIS CITY?

I WILL MAKE THE LIONS ROAR AND CREATE PANIC AND CHAOS AMONG THE PEOPLE. THEN I WILL MARCH INTO THE CITY.

OH! SO THAT'S IT!

IMPOSSIBLE! THESE NOBLE CREATURES WILL NEVER OBEY A COMMON JACKAL.

THAT'S WHAT YOU THINK! THE LIONS WILL ALL OBEY ME. EVEN THIS LION ON WHOSE BACK I SIT WILL ROAR.

DON'T BRAG. GET HIM TO ROAR—IF YOU CAN.

OBEY YOUR KING! ROAR WITH ALL YOUR MIGHT!

GRR-RR! GRR-R-R!

THE LION ROARED AND ROARED. TERRIFIED, THE ELEPHANTS SHOOK OFF THE LION. THE JACKALS CRASHED TO THE GROUND.

SEEING THE ELEPHANTS RUN AMUCK, ALL THE ANIMALS BROKE INTO A STAMPEDE AND RAN HELTER SKELTER.

IN THE STAMPEDE, THE JACKALS WERE TRAMPLED TO DEATH.

THAT WAS THE END OF KING SARVADATA WHO HAD DARED TO DREAM OF CONQUERING VARANASI.

THE JACKAL AND THE OTTERS

A JACKAL'S WIFE ONCE WANTED TO EAT SOME FRESH ROHITA FISH. PROMISING TO BRING IT FOR HER, THE JACKAL WENT TO THE RIVER.

I'VE PROMISED TO BRING HER THE FISH. BUT HOW AM I GOING TO DO IT?

JUST THEN HE SAW TWO OTTERS DRAGGING ALONG A HUGE ROHITA FISH.

THIS FISH SHOULD LAST US A LONG TIME.

THE JACKAL DREW NEARER.

YES, BUT HOW SHALL WE DIVIDE IT?

IF I DIVIDE IT, I'LL HAVE TO GIVE HIM THE LARGER SHARE.

YOU DIVIDE IT.

IF I DIVIDE IT, I'LL HAVE TO GIVE HIM THE BEST BITS.

NO, YOU DIVIDE IT.

NO, YOU DIVIDE IT.

HERE'S MY CHANCE! THEY'RE SURE TO ASK ME TO DIVIDE IT FOR THEM.

THE JACKAL THEN CUT OFF THE HEAD AND THE TAIL OF THE FISH.

THE JACKAL AND THE SHE-GOAT

LONG AGO, IN A CAVE ON THE SLOPES OF THE HIMALAYAS, THERE LIVED A HERD OF WILD GOATS. ONE DAY, AS A JACKAL AND HIS MATE WERE PROWLING ABOUT FOR FOOD, THEY SAW THE GOATS GRAZING.

COME! LET US KILL ONE OF THEM.

WAIT! IF WE ARE CLEVER, WE'LL HAVE FOOD ENOUGH FOR MANY MONTHS.

THEY WAITED TILL THE GOATS BEGAN TO WANDER APART AS THEY GRAZED.

LET'S FOLLOW THAT ONE TILL HE IS FAR AWAY FROM THE OTHERS.

A FEW HOURS LATER —

THERE! I'VE KILLED HIM. NOW HELP ME DRAG HIM TO OUR CAVE.

MANY MONTHS PASSED AND, ONE BY ONE, THE GOATS WERE EATEN BY THE JACKALS.

THE ONLY ONE LEFT WAS A WISE SHE-GOAT.

I DARE NOT GO OUT. THE JACKALS ARE ABOUT AGAIN!

THAT SHE-GOAT SEEMS TO BE WISE TO US. SHE DOES NOT COME OUT AT ALL.

THE JACKAL HAD AN IDEA.

YOU GO ALONE EVERY DAY AND TRY TO WIN HER CONFIDENCE. WHEN SHE BEGINS TO TRUST YOU I WILL LIE OUTSIDE OUR CAVE AND PRETEND TO BE DEAD. AND YOU... BZZ. BZZ....

EAGER TO CARRY OUT THE PLAN, THE SHE-JACKAL HASTENED TO THE GOAT'S CAVE.

O WISE GOAT, DO YOU LIVE HERE ALL ALONE?

IT'S THE WIFE OF THE JACKAL!

PLEASE DON'T BE AFRAID. I'VE COME TO MAKE FRIENDS WITH YOU. PLEASE COME OUT.

NO! I DON'T TRUST YOU. GO AWAY. YOU KILLED ALL MY RELATIVES.

IT WAS MY HUSBAND, NOT ME. IF YOU DON'T TRUST ME, YOU NEEDN'T COME OUT. BUT, PLEASE, DON'T REFUSE TO TALK TO ME.

THERE'S NO HARM IN SPEAKING TO HER FROM INSIDE. SHE MAY BE INNOCENT.

I AM VERY UNHAPPY. NO ONE IS WILLING TO BE MY FRIEND, BECAUSE OF MY HUSBAND'S EVIL WAYS.

THE KIND-HEARTED GOAT FELT SORRY FOR THE SHE-JACKAL.

PLEASE DON'T SAY THAT. I'LL BE YOUR FRIEND.

AS EACH DAY PASSED THE SHE-GOAT'S TRUST IN THE JACKAL INCREASED, TILL ONE DAY—

TOMORROW WE SHALL CARRY OUT THE NEXT PART OF OUR PLAN.

THE NEXT DAY—

OH, I AM LEFT ALL ALONE! MY HUSBAND IS DEAD. PLEASE COME AND HELP ME BURY HIM.

NO! NO! I CANNOT COME. I'M AFRAID OF HIM.

BUT WHAT HARM CAN HE DO TO YOU NOW THAT HE IS DEAD?

DEAD OR ALIVE, HE'S CRUEL AND I'M AFRAID TO COME OUT.

AND I HAD THOUGHT YOU WERE MY FRIEND! HOW UNFORTUNATE I AM THAT I MUST BURY MY HUSBAND ALL BY MYSELF!

SHE CAN'T BE LYING. HE MUST REALLY BE DEAD.

DON'T WEEP, MY FRIEND. I'LL COME WITH YOU.

AS THEY WERE ABOUT TO SET OUT, HOWEVER, THE SHE-GOAT SUDDENLY BECAME DOUBTFUL AGAIN.

FRIEND, YOU WALK AHEAD AND SHOW ME THE WAY. I'LL FOLLOW.

A LITTLE LATER—

AH, FOOTSTEPS! HERE THEY COME.

HE FORGOT THAT HE WAS SUPPOSED TO PLAY DEAD, AND OPENED HIS EYES TO LOOK AT THE PLUMP GOAT.

HE'S ALIVE!

THE WICKED WRETCH WANTS TO KILL ME. THEY ARE BOTH TRAITORS!

WHEN SHE HAD GONE —

HUMPH! I THOUGHT YOU HAD WON HER CONFIDENCE!

I HAD! BUT YOU, MY LORD, HAD TO BE A FOOL AND SPOIL IT ALL.

THE JACKAL WAS SO CRESTFALLEN THAT HIS MATE FELT SORRY FOR HIM.

DON'T LOOK SO UNHAPPY! I'LL BRING HER AGAIN. THIS TIME, BE ON YOUR GUARD.

AH! MY FRIEND, YOU HAVE PERFORMED A MIRACLE! AS YOU CAME NEAR HIM, MY HUSBAND CAME TO LIFE AGAIN. HE WANTS TO MEET YOU AND THANK YOU.

THE TRAITOR! SHE TAKES ME TO BE A TRUSTING FOOL. I'LL TEACH HER A LESSON SHE'LL NEVER FORGET!

THE SHE-GOAT CAME OUT.

ALL RIGHT, I'LL COME — WITH AN ESCORT OF TWO THOUSAND DOGS. IF THEY DO NOT FIND ENOUGH FOOD, THEY WILL DEVOUR YOU AND YOUR MATE. SO HURRY HOME AND PREPARE ENOUGH FOOD FOR US ALL!

THE RUSE WORKED.

TWO THOUSAND DOGS! I'VE HAD ENOUGH OF THIS GOAT.

DEAR FRIEND, I'VE CHANGED MY MIND. YOU'D BETTER NOT COME. YOUR CAVE MIGHT BE BURGLED WHILE YOU ARE AWAY.

BUT I WANT TO COME AND....

NO! PLEASE DON'T BOTHER. SOME OTHER TIME, PERHAPS.

THEN SHE RAN FOR HER LIFE...

...TILL SHE REACHED HER MATE.

QUICK! WE MUST RUN. OR ELSE WE'LL MAKE A MEAL FOR TWO THOUSAND DOGS!

TWO THOUSAND DOGS!

THE JACKAL AND HIS MATE TOOK TO THEIR HEELS, AND THEY WERE NOT SEEN OR HEARD OF EVER AGAIN.

Couldn't find the
Amar Chitra Katha
title you wanted
in the store next door?

Log on to **www.theackshop.com** where ALL the titles are just a click away

90 million copies of over 400
titles sold in the last 40 years

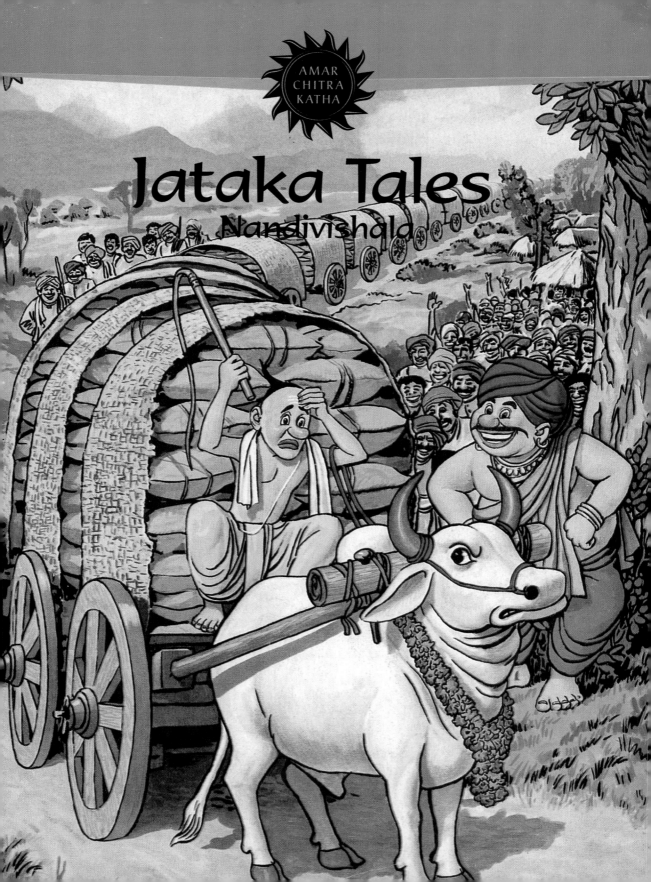

Jataka Tales

Nandivishala

Illustrated Classics From India

Jataka Tales
Nandivishala

All living creatures die to be born again, so the Hindus believe. Siddhartha, who became the Buddha, was no exception. It is believed that several lifetimes as a Bodhisattva go into the making of Buddha, the Enlightened One. The Bodhisattva is one, who by performing virtuous, kind and intelligent acts, aspires to become a Buddha. The Bodhisattva came in many forms – man, monkey, deer, elephant, lion. Whatever his mortal body, he spreads the message of justice and wisdom, tempered with compassion.

This wisdom, the wisdom of right thinking and right living, is preserved in the Jataka stories. The Jataka tales, on which the present title is based, is a collection of 550 stories included in the Pali canon. These are based on folklore, legends and ballads of ancient India. We cannot assign a definite date to the Jataka stories. Taking into account archaeological and literary evidence, it seems likely that they were compiled in the period between 3rd century BC and 5th century AD. The Jataka tales provide invaluable information about ancient Indian civilisation, culture and philosophy.

Script: Lopa Mudra   Illustrations: Ashok Dongre   Cover: C. M. Vitankar

NANDI VISHALA

A BRAHMAN ONCE RECEIVED THE GIFT OF A BULL—CALF WHOM HE NAMED NANDI VISHALA.

HE LOOKED AFTER IT WELL, AND IT GREW INTO A FINE, STURDY BULL.

THE KIND BRAHMAN HAS BROUGHT ME UP WITH LOVING CARE, AS IF I WERE HIS OWN SON. I MUST REPAY HIM FOR ALL HIS TROUBLE.

ONE DAY—

GO TO A RICH MERCHANT. TELL HIM THAT YOUR BULL CAN DRAW A HUNDRED LOADED CARTS. MAKE A BET ON THAT FOR A THOUSAND PIECES OF GOLD.

THE BRAHMAN COULD NOT BELIEVE HIS EARS.

AM I DREAMING OR HAVE I GONE MAD? I HEARD MY BULL TALKING!

YOU ARE NOT DREAMING, MASTER. DO AS I SAY. IT WILL BRING YOU GOOD FORTUNE.

ARE YOU SURE I'LL WIN SUCH A BET?

OF COURSE! OR I WOULDN'T HAVE SUGGESTED IT.

SO THE BRAHMAN WENT TO A RICH MERCHANT.

SIR, WHOSE BULL DO YOU THINK IS THE STRONGEST IN THIS TOWN?

THERE ARE MANY STRONG BULLS IN THIS TOWN BUT MINE ARE THE STRONGEST.

WELL, I HAVE A BULL WHO CAN PULL A HUNDRED LOADED CARTS. CAN YOURS DO BETTER THAN THAT?

THE MERCHANT LAUGHED—

YOU MUST BE JOKING!

I'M NOT!

IT'S IMPOSSIBLE! NO BULL CAN DRAW A HUNDRED LOADED CARTS. I'M WILLING TO MAKE A WAGER ON THAT.

THE STAKE SHALL BE A THOUSAND PIECES OF GOLD!

AGREED!

ON THE APPOINTED DAY, THE BRAHMAN WAS READY WITH A HUNDRED CARTS LOADED WITH SAND, GRAVEL AND STONES.

A THOUSAND PIECES OF GOLD WILL SOON BE MINE! ADD TO THAT THE THOUSAND I'VE SAVED OVER THE PAST FEW YEARS AND I'LL HAVE TWO THOUSAND PIECES OF GOLD!

HANGING A GARLAND ROUND NANDI VISHALA'S NECK, HE YOKED HIM TO THE FIRST CART.

WITH THAT MONEY, I'LL BUY MANY MORE BULLS AND MAKE MANY MORE WAGERS TILL I BECOME THE RICHEST MAN IN TOWN! EVERYONE WILL HAVE TO BOW TO MY WISHES!

THESE THOUGHTS MADE THE BRAHMAN VERY ARROGANT AND QUITE UNLIKE HIS USUAL SELF.

COME ON, YOU RASCAL! PULL! BE QUICK, YOU RASCAL!

THE BULL WAS SHOCKED BY HIS BELOVED MASTER'S WORDS AND BEHAVIOUR.

WELL, I'M NOT THE RASCAL HE CALLS TO! I WON'T MOVE!

THE BRAHMAN BECAME FRANTIC.

WHAT'S WRONG WITH NANDI VISHALA? WHY DOES HE IGNORE MY ORDERS?

THE MERCHANT WAS JUBILANT.

HA! HA! COME ON, SIR! YOU'VE LOST A THOUSAND GOLD PIECES!

THE BRAHMAN HAD TO GO AND BRING THE GOLD HE HAD KEPT HIDDEN AT HOME.

ALL MY LIFE'S SAVINGS GONE!

UNYOKING NANDI VISHALA, HE SADLY WALKED AWAY.

LATER, AT HOME —

ARE YOU ASLEEP, SIR?

HOW CAN I SLEEP WHEN I'VE LOST ALL MY SAVINGS? I SHOULD NEVER HAVE LISTENED TO YOU!

WHY DID YOU CALL ME A RASCAL? HAVE I EVER BROKEN A POT OR GORED ANYONE OR...?

NO, NEVER, MY CHILD!

NANDI VISHALA IMMEDIATELY FELT SORRY FOR THE BRAHMAN.

ALL IS NOT YET LOST. GO AND MAKE THE WAGER AGAIN. LET THE STAKE BE 2000 PIECES OF GOLD THIS TIME. ONLY REMEMBER, DON'T EVER CALL ME A RASCAL AGAIN!

THE BRAHMAN WENT TO THE MERCHANT AND OFFERED TO MAKE THE SAME WAGER AS BEFORE —

THE MAN SEEMS TO BE A FOOL!

YOU ARE NOT CONTENT WITH LOSING A THOUSAND PIECES OF GOLD!

I AM SO CERTAIN OF WINNING THAT I'M WILLING TO BET TWO THOUSAND THIS TIME.

TWO THOUSAND! ALL RIGHT, I ACCEPT!

WHEN THE LOADED CARTS AND THE BULL WERE READY —

NOW THEN, MY FINE FELLOW! PULL THE CARTS ALONG.

WITH A SINGLE TUG, NANDI VISHALA PULLED THE CARTS...

... TILL THE LAST ONE STOOD WHERE THE FIRST HAD BEEN!

AMAZING!

YOU DESERVE EVERY ONE OF THESE GOLD PIECES!

THE BRAHMAN TOOK THE TWO THOUSAND PIECES OF GOLD AND HE WENT HOME A HAPPIER, RICHER, WISER MAN.

THE SERVANT AND THE TREASURE

ONCE THERE WERE TWO OLD LANDOWNERS WHO WERE FRIENDS. ONE OF THEM HAD A VERY YOUNG WIFE WHO HAD RECENTLY BORNE HIM A SON.

YOU ARE VERY LUCKY. YOU HAVE A SON AND HEIR TO WHOM YOU CAN BEQUEATH YOUR FORTUNE.

YES, I'M INDEED LUCKY.

BUT I, TOO, HAVE WORRIES. IF I DIE, MY SON MAY NEVER GET THE MONEY.

WOULDN'T THE SAFEST COURSE BE TO BURY MY MONEY IN THE FOREST?

IT WOULD CERTAINLY BE A WISE THING TO DO.

SO, TAKING A HOUSEHOLD SERVANT CALLED NANDA INTO HIS CONFIDENCE, THE LANDOWNER WENT TO A NEARBY FOREST AND BURIED HIS TREASURE AT A CERTAIN SPOT.

MY GOOD NANDA, WHEN MY SON COMES OF AGE, SHOW HIM THIS TREASURE. NO ONE ELSE SHOULD BE TOLD ABOUT IT.

THE OLD MAN DIED SOON AFTER. MANY YEARS LATER, HIS SON, NOW A YOUNG MAN, MET HIS FATHER'S FRIEND.

MY FATHER WAS A RICH MAN. BUT THERE DOESN'T SEEM TO BE ENOUGH MONEY LEFT TO MANAGE THE ESTATE.

BUT HE DID LEAVE A LOT OF MONEY FOR YOU, SON. DIDN'T YOU KNOW THAT?

NO! WHERE IS IT?

SOMEWHERE IN THE FOREST. ASK YOUR SERVANT, NANDA. HE KNOWS ALL ABOUT IT.

THE YOUNG MAN WENT TO NANDA.

DO YOU KNOW WHERE MY FATHER PUT HIS TREASURE?

YES, MASTER. IT'S BURIED IN THE FOREST.

WELL THEN, LET'S GO AND GET IT. I NEED IT NOW.

I'LL TAKE YOU THERE, MASTER.

SOON THEY WERE ON THEIR WAY TO THE FOREST.

NANDA IS AN HONEST MAN. HE COULD EASILY HAVE TAKEN THE TREASURE FOR HIMSELF.

WHEN THEY REACHED THE MIDDLE OF THE FOREST —

WELL, NANDA, WHERE IS THE MONEY?

SUDDENLY NANDA WHO HAD BEEN DOCILE FOR YEARS, TURNED ARROGANT AND INSOLENT.

WHAT MAKES YOU THINK THERE IS MONEY BURIED HERE FOR YOU?

THE YOUNG MAN WAS TAKEN ABACK.

WHAT'S WRONG WITH HIM? I DON'T UNDERSTAND. WHAT SHALL I DO?

I KNOW! I'LL PRETEND I DIDN'T HEAR A WORD!

HE TURNED CALMLY TO NANDA.

ALL RIGHT. LET'S GO HOME THEN.

WHAT A RELIEF! HE'S FOLLOWING ME QUIETLY.

A FEW DAYS LATER, THEY RETURNED TO THE FOREST.

STRANGE! HE DIDN'T SEEM TO HESITATE.

BUT WHEN THEY REACHED THE SAME SPOT —

YOU IDIOT! WHAT DO YOU HOPE TO FIND HERE?

ONCE AGAIN THE YOUNG MAN IGNORED NANDA'S INSOLENCE.

NOTHING! LET'S GO HOME.

WHEN WE SET OUT, I AM CERTAIN THAT NANDA MEANS TO SHOW ME WHERE THE TREASURE IS. BUT, LATER, HE BEGINS TO ABUSE ME. WHAT COULD THE REASON FOR THIS BE?

MY FATHER'S WISE OLD FRIEND SHOULD BE ABLE TO HELP.

SO HE WENT TO THE OLD MAN AND DESCRIBED NANDA'S STRANGE BEHAVIOUR.

IT'S SIMPLE! YOU SAY HE STARTS ABUSING YOU WHEN YOU REACH A PARTICULAR SPOT IN THE FOREST? THEN THAT'S WHERE THE TREASURE IS BURIED!

HOW DO YOU KNOW?

MONEY CAN CORRUPT EVEN AN HONEST MAN. THE MOMENT NANDA STANDS ON THE SPOT WHERE THE TREASURE IS BURIED, HE BECOMES A DIFFERENT MAN.

IF THAT IS SO, WHY DIDN'T HE TAKE IT FOR HIMSELF?

BECAUSE HE DIDN'T DARE!

13

WHAT SHOULD I DO NOW?

GO BACK TO THE FOREST WITH HIM AND WHEN HE STARTS SHOUTING, YOU....

AND THE OLD MAN TOLD THE YOUNG ONE WHAT HE SHOULD DO.

THE NEXT DAY, THE YOUNG MAN WENT TO THE FOREST WITH NANDA AGAIN. AT THE SAME SPOT, NANDA BEGAN TO ABUSE HIM.

YOU FOOL! YOU IDIOT! YOU....

BUT THIS TIME HIS YOUNG MASTER KNEW WHAT TO DO.

WHO DO YOU THINK YOU ARE TALKING TO, YOU KNAVE?

HE BEGAN TO DIG AS NANDA WATCHED HIM DUMBLY.

DON'T MOVE FROM THERE, TILL I ORDER YOU TO DO SO.

SOON —

THERE! I'VE FOUND IT!

COME HERE! CARRY THIS HOME ON YOUR HEAD.

NANDA OBEYED MEEKLY.

THE SON TOOK HIS TREASURE HOME. AND NANDA SERVED HIM FAITHFULLY TILL HIS DYING DAY.

THE WISE ONE'S ADVICE WORKED! HOW GRATEFUL I AM TO MY FATHER'S FRIEND!

THE HYPOCRITICAL SADHU

A RASCAL OF A SADHU LIVED IN A FOREST HERMITAGE ON THE OUTSKIRTS OF A VILLAGE AND HAD WON THE TRUST OF A ZAMINDAR.

NOW, THE ZAMINDAR HAD SOME GOLD WHICH HE WANTED TO HIDE FROM ROBBERS. AS HE WONDERED WHERE TO PUT IT —

I KNOW WHAT! THE SADHU IS A MODEL OF GOODNESS... AND DACOITS WOULD NEVER ATTACK A HERMITAGE!

SO HE WENT WITH HIS GOLD TO THE HERMITAGE.

HOLY SIR! WE ZAMINDARS LIVE IN CONSTANT FEAR OF ROBBERS. SO I AM GOING TO BURY MY GOLD RIGHT HERE IN YOUR HERMITAGE.

THERE'S ENOUGH GOLD THERE TO KEEP ME HAPPY FOR THE REST OF MY LIFE!

I AM LEAVING MY GOLD BURIED HERE AS I HAVE COMPLETE FAITH IN YOU. PLEASE DON'T LET ME DOWN.

IT'S NOT NECESSARY TO TELL ME THAT. WE, WHO HAVE GIVEN UP THE WORLD, NEVER COVET ANOTHER'S PROPERTY!

A FEW DAYS LATER, THE RASCAL REMOVED THE GOLD AND BURIED IT AGAIN AT ANOTHER SPOT A SHORT DISTANCE AWAY.

TOMORROW I SHALL GO AND TAKE MY LEAVE OF THE ZAMINDAR.

THE NEXT DAY —

I HAVE DECIDED TO GO AWAY FROM HERE.

WHAT'S THE MATTER? HAVE I DISPLEASED YOU IN ANY WAY?

NO, THAT'S NOT THE REASON. HE WHO HAS RENOUNCED THE WORLD SHOULD NOT LIVE IN ONE PLACE FOR TOO LONG. IT IS FORBIDDEN. SO I MUST TAKE MY LEAVE OF YOU.

WELL, IF YOU MUST GO, I CANNOT STOP YOU.

THE ZAMINDAR WALKED SOME DISTANCE WITH THE SADHU. THEN HE REVERENTLY BADE HIM GOOD BYE.

WHEN THE ZAMINDAR HAD LEFT, A THOUGHT SUDDENLY STRUCK THE SADHU —

I MUST MAKE SURE HE DOES NOT SUSPECT ME WHEN HE FINDS HIS GOLD HAS BEEN STOLEN. OUR PATHS MAY CROSS IN THE FUTURE.

PICKING UP A STRAW AND...

...STICKING IT IN HIS HAIR...

...HE RETRACED HIS STEPS.

A LITTLE LATER, AS THE ZAMINDAR SAT TALKING WITH A MERCHANT WHO HAD COME TO VISIT HIM, THE SADHU WALKED IN.

WELCOME, HOLY ONE! WHAT BRINGS YOU BACK? HAVE YOU CHANGED YOUR MIND?

NO, BUT A STRAW FROM YOUR ROOF HAD STUCK IN MY HAIR. SINCE WE SADHUS MAY NOT TAKE ANYTHING WHICH IS NOT BESTOWED ON US, I HAVE BROUGHT IT BACK TO YOU.

THE MERCHANT, HOWEVER, WAS A SHREWD MAN.

COME TO RETURN A STRAW INDEED! THIS FELLOW HAS ROBBED THE ZAMINDAR OF SOMETHING, I AM CERTAIN!

BUT THE ZAMINDAR WAS TAKEN IN.

WHAT A SENSITIVE MAN! WHY, HE WON'T TAKE SO MUCH AS A STRAW WHICH DOES NOT BELONG TO HIM!

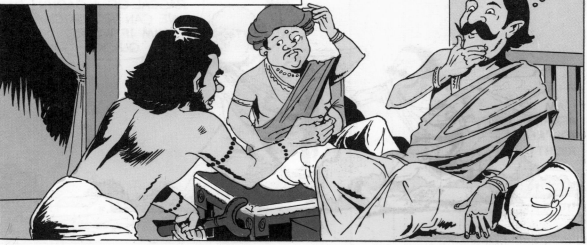

THROW AWAY THE STRAW AND GO YOUR WAY, HOLY ONE.

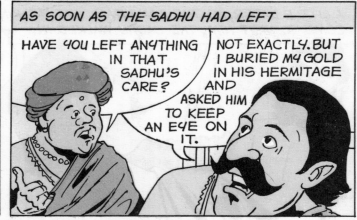

AS SOON AS THE SADHU HAD LEFT ——

HAVE YOU LEFT ANYTHING IN THAT SADHU'S CARE?

NOT EXACTLY. BUT I BURIED MY GOLD IN HIS HERMITAGE AND ASKED HIM TO KEEP AN EYE ON IT.

WELL, JUST GO AND SEE IF IT IS STILL THERE.

THE ZAMINDAR WENT AND SOON RETURNED.

IT'S NOT THERE! IT'S BEEN STOLEN!

THE THIEF IS NONE OTHER THAN THAT RASCAL OF A SADHU! WE CAN YET CATCH HIM IF WE'RE QUICK.

I AM AFRAID YOU'RE RIGHT!

SOON ——

THERE HE IS!

THE MERCHANT WAS THE FIRST TO REACH HIM —

CAUGHT YOU, YOU ROGUE!

WH—WHAT? I AM A HOLY MAN WHO HAS RENOUNCED THE WORLD....

IF YOU DON'T TELL US WHERE YOU'VE HIDDEN THE MONEY, YOU'LL SOON HAVE TO RENOUNCE YOUR LIFE!

MERCY, MERCY! I'LL TELL YOU WHERE IT IS!

THE SADHU SHOWED THEM WHERE HE HAD HIDDEN THE GOLD.

SO, THE STOLEN GOLD DIDN'T TROUBLE YOUR CONSCIENCE AS MUCH AS A STRAW DID!

AND GIVING THE SADHU A SOUND SCOLDING, THEY LET HIM GO.

WHAT'S IN A NAME?

IN TAKSHASHILA, THERE ONCE LIVED A VEDIC SCHOLAR WHO HAD FIVE HUNDRED YOUNG DISCIPLES.

ONE OF THEM WAS GIVEN THE NAME 'LOWLY' WHEN HE BECAME A STUDENT.

LOWLY, CAN YOU HELP ME WITH THIS SHLOKA* ? I CAN'T SEEM TO GET IT RIGHT.

EH? OH! IT'S EASY. I'LL HELP YOU.

LOWLY, WILL YOU HELP ME CARRY THIS ?

EH! AH! TO BE SURE, I WILL.

SO HELPFUL AND KIND WAS **LOWLY** THAT ALL HIS FELLOW STUDENTS LIKED HIM.

✳ A SANSKRIT VERSE

22

BUT HE WAS NOT HAPPY.

WHY HAVE I BEEN GIVEN SUCH A NAME? EVERY TIME I HEAR IT, I FEEL SAD.

SO, ONE DAY, HE WENT TO HIS TEACHER.

SIR, PLEASE GIVE ME A NEW NAME WHICH SOUNDS MORE RESPECTABLE.

ALL RIGHT, MY SON. GO, TRAVEL THROUGH THE LAND WHEREVER YOUR FANCY TAKES YOU. THEN COME BACK AND I WILL CHANGE YOUR NAME FOR YOU.

SO LOWLY WANDERED FROM VILLAGE TO VILLAGE...

...TILL HE CAME TO THE OUTSKIRTS OF A CITY. THERE HE SAW A DEAD BODY BEING CARRIED BY PALLBEARERS.

WHAT WAS THAT MAN CALLED?

HIS NAME WAS 'LIFE', SIR.

WHAT? CAN 'LIFE' BE DEAD?

WHY NOT? WHETHER HE WAS CALLED 'LIFE' OR 'DEATH', HE WOULD HAVE HAD TO DIE ALL THE SAME! A NAME ONLY SERVES TO MARK WHO'S WHO! YOU SEEM TO BE A FOOL!

PONDERING OVER THE MATTER, LOWLY ENTERED THE CITY.

SUDDENLY —

MERCY! MERCY, MY MISTRESS! I'LL TRY AND DO BETTER TOMORROW.

MOVED BY THE SIGHT, KIND LOWLY INTERVENED.

WAIT, MY GOOD WOMAN! WHY DO YOU WHIP THE POOR GIRL?

SHE IS MY SLAVE. I SENT HER OUT TO EARN MONEY AND SHE HAS COME BACK EMPTY-HANDED!

LOWLY TOOK OUT A COIN AND GAVE IT TO THE WOMAN.

HERE. KEEP THIS AND SPARE THE GIRL. SHE'LL DO BETTER TOMORROW.

AS LOWLY WALKED AWAY HE SPOKE TO A PASSERBY WHO HAD WITNESSED THE SCENE.

POOR GIRL! SHE MUST HAVE AN ACCURSED NAME!

SHE IS CALLED 'RICH'!

WHAT! AND WITH A NAME LIKE THAT SHE COULD NOT EVEN EARN A DAY'S PALTRY WAGES!

YOU SEEM TO BE A FOOL! A NAME ONLY SERVES TO MARK WHO'S WHO AND NOT WHAT THEY ARE.

PERHAPS HE'S RIGHT. YET....

MORE RECONCILED TO HIS NAME, LOWLY NOW LEFT THE CITY AND TOOK THE ROAD BACK TOWARDS TAKSHASHILA.

25

ON THE WAY —

I AM GOING TO TAKSHASHILA BUT I HAVE LOST MY WAY. CAN YOU HELP ME?

I AM GOING THERE MYSELF. YOU CAN COME WITH ME.

AFTER THEY HAD GONE A LITTLE WAY —

WHAT IS YOUR NAME, FRIEND?

I AM CALLED 'GUIDE'.

'GUIDE'? AND YOU'VE LOST YOUR WAY?

ARE YOU MAKING FUN OF ME? WHETHER ONE'S NAME IS 'GUIDE' OR 'MISGUIDE', ONE CAN LOSE ONE'S WAY ALL THE SAME!

EVERYONE KNOWS THAT NAMES ONLY SERVE TO MARK WHO'S WHO AND NOT WHAT THEY ARE.

YES, I HAVE AT LAST COME TO UNDERSTAND THAT TRUTH.

AT TAKSHASHILA, LOWLY WENT DIRECTLY TO HIS TEACHER.

WELL, DO YOU STILL WANT TO CHANGE YOUR NAME?

MASTER, I FIND THAT DEATH CAN COME TO 'LIFE', THAT 'RICH' AND 'POOR' MAY BOTH BE POOR, AND THAT 'GUIDE' AND 'MISGUIDE' CAN LOSE THEIR WAY.

I KNOW NOW THAT A NAME SERVES ONLY TO TELL WHO IS WHO AND DOES NOT GOVERN THE OWNER'S DESTINY. I AM QUITE CONTENT WITH MY OWN NAME AND DO NOT WANT TO CHANGE IT FOR ANOTHER.

THE MOST VIRTUOUS STUDENT

IN VARANASI, THERE ONCE LIVED A RENOWNED SCHOLAR WHO HAD A GROWN-UP DAUGHTER.

HE HAD A LARGE NUMBER OF YOUNG STUDENTS IN HIS CARE. ONE DAY, AN IDEA STRUCK HIM —

I WILL PUT MY STUDENTS THROUGH A TEST TO FIND OUT WHICH IS THE MOST VIRTUOUS OF THEM.

THE NEXT DAY —

I CANNOT AFFORD THE CLOTHES AND ORNAMENTS REQUIRED FOR MY DAUGHTER'S MARRIAGE. WILL YOU, MY BOYS, HELP ME OUT BY STEALING THESE THINGS FOR ME?

BUT NO ONE SHOULD SEE YOU STEALING. IT SHOULD BE DONE IN THE STRICTEST SECRECY. ONLY THEN WILL I ACCEPT WHAT YOU BRING.

FROM THAT DAY ONWARDS, THE STUDENTS STOLE VALUABLES FROM THEIR FAMILIES AND FRIENDS...

...AND BROUGHT THEM SECRETLY TO THEIR TEACHER.

I MUST KEEP WHAT EACH ONE BRINGS IN SEPARATE LOTS, SO THAT THEY CAN BE EASILY RETURNED TO THEIR OWNERS.

THE TEACHER WAS OVERJOYED.

I HAVE FOUND THE BOY FOR MY DAUGHTER! OF ALL MY STUDENTS, HE IS THE ONLY ONE WHO IS VIRTUOUS!

MY SON, I HAVE NO NEED OF WEALTH. I HAD ONLY ASKED YOU TO STEAL AS A TEST TO FIND A VIRTUOUS MAN FOR MY DAUGHTER. YOU ALONE ARE WORTHY OF HER.

THEN HE SENT FOR ALL THE OTHER BOYS.

STEALING, EVEN FOR A GOOD CAUSE, IS WRONG. YOU HAVE FAILED THE TEST OF VIRTUE. YOU MUST NOW RETURN ALL THAT YOU HAVE STOLEN TO THE OWNERS.

THEN, ADORNING HIS DAUGHTER WITH JEWELS, HE GAVE HER IN MARRIAGE TO THE VIRTUOUS STUDENT.

THEY'RE COMING!

" Your favourite characters delivered
at your doorstep, anywhere in the world,
BEFORE they reach the newsstands!* "

Subscribe to **TINKLE** today and make sure
you never miss an issue!

Illustrated Classics From India

Jataka Tales
Bird Stories

All living creatures die to be born again, so the Hindus believe. Siddhartha, who became the Buddha, was no exception. It is believed that several lifetimes as a Bodhisattva go into the making of a Buddha, the Enlightened One. The Bodhisattva is one, who by performing virtuous, kind and intelligent acts, aspires to become a Buddha. The Bodhisattva came in many forms – man, monkey, deer, elephant, lion. Whatever his mortal body, he spreads the message of justice and wisdom, tempered with compassion.

This wisdom, the wisdom of right thinking and right living, is preserved in the Jataka stories. The Jataka tales, on which the present title is based, is a collection of 550 stories included in the Pali canon. These are based on folklore, legends and ballads of ancient India. We cannot assign a definite date to the Jataka stories. Taking into account archaeological and literary evidence, it seems likely that they were compiled in the period between 3rd century BC and 5th century AD. The Jataka tales provide invaluable information about ancient Indian civilisation, culture and philosophy.

This volume of bird stories that deals with issues of friendship, greed and loyalty, will keep the children amused, while never failing to point out the ultimate triumph of good over evil.

Editor: Anant Pai

Script: Kamala Chandrakant   **Illustrations: Ashok Dongre**   **Cover: C. M. Vitankar**

THE VALUE OF FRIENDS

LONG AGO, ON THE SHORE OF A LARGE LAKE, THERE LIVED A HAWK.

THEN ONE DAY, A SHE-HAWK CAME TO LIVE ON THE OPPOSITE SHORE. WHEN THE HAWK HEARD OF IT HE FLEW OVER TO HER.

WILL YOU BE MY WIFE? TOGETHER WE COULD RAISE A FINE FAMILY

ALL RIGHT. BUT TELL ME, DO YOU HAVE ANY FRIENDS?

NO.

THEN YOU MUST MAKE SOME FRIENDS. IN TIMES OF NEED, IT IS FRIENDS WHO HELP.

I DON'T NEED FRIENDS. BUT I'LL DO AS YOU SAY. WHO SHALL WE START WITH?

OUR NEIGHBOURS, OF COURSE! GO AND CALL ON THE LION, THE OSPREY AND THE TORTOISE!

THE HAWK AGREED AND FLEW TO THE TINY ISLAND IN THE MIDDLE OF THE LAKE WHERE THE TORTOISE DWELT.

O, TORTOISE, ACCEPT ME AS YOUR FRIEND.

WITH PLEASURE!

HE THEN MADE FRIENDS WITH THE OSPREY.

ANY TIME YOU NEED ME, SEND FOR ME.

FINALLY, THE HAWK CALLED ON THE LION —

NOW THAT YOU ARE MY FRIEND, NO ONE WILL HARM YOU.

THE HAWK THEN RETURNED TO THE SHE-HAWK.

I HAVE THREE FRIENDS NOW.

AH! NOW WE CAN DECIDE WHERE TO MAKE OUR HOME.

WHAT ABOUT THE KADAMBA TREE ON THE ISLAND WHERE THE TORTOISE LIVES?

THAT'S A GOOD IDEA.

SO THE TWO FLEW OVER TO THE ISLAND AND MADE A NEST ON THE KADAMBA TREE. SOON TWO LITTLE ONES WERE BORN TO THEM.

THIS IS THE SAFEST PLACE WE COULD FIND —FAR FROM THE HAUNTS OF MEN.

BUT THE PLACE WAS NOT AS SAFE AS THE HAWKS IMAGINED. ONE DAY TWO HUNTERS CAME —

IT'S BEEN A BAD DAY. WE'VE CAUGHT NOTHING, NOT EVEN A RABBIT!

AND IT'S ALMOST EVENING!

WE CAN'T RETURN EMPTY-HANDED!

WE MIGHT YET CATCH A FISH OR A YOUNG TORTOISE, PER-HAPS.

BUT THEY HAD NO LUCK. TOWARDS NIGHTFALL —

WHAT SHALL WE DO?

LET'S SWIM ACROSS TO THAT ISLAND, AND SPEND THE NIGHT THERE. AT DAWN WE'LL TRY OUR LUCK AGAIN.

WHEN THEY REACHED THE ISLAND —

THESE MOSQUITOES ARE IMPOSSIBLE!

LET'S LIGHT A FIRE. THAT SHOULD DRIVE THEM AWAY.

CHEEP CHEEP

DID YOU HEAR THAT?

I DID! FLEDGLINGS! ON THIS TREE!

DID YOU HEAR THAT? HUMAN VOICES!

SH-S-SH! LET'S FIND OUT WHAT THEY ARE PLANNING.

THEY ARE PLANNING TO EAT OUR CHILDREN! FRIEND TORTOISE IS ASLEEP. QUICK, MY DEAR, FLY TO THE OSPREY AND SEEK HIS HELP.

THE OSPREY WAS SURPRISED TO SEE THE HAWK.

WHAT BRINGS YOU HERE AT THIS HOUR?

WHEN THE HAWK TOLD HIM —

HAVE THEY CLIMBED THE TREE YET?

NOT YET. THEY'RE BUSY LIGHTING A FIRE.

THEN FLY BACK TO YOUR WIFE AND COMFORT HER. I'LL TAKE CARE OF THE HUNTERS.

UNDER COVER OF NIGHT, THE OSPREY FLEW TO THE KADAMBA TREE AND WAITED AND WATCHED.

THERE! THE FIRE IS BLAZING MERRILY. LET'S GET THE BIRDS.

NOW TO PUT MY PLAN INTO ACTION!

SUDDENLY THE OSPREY DIVED INTO THE LAKE...

...CAME OUT, SHOOK HIMSELF OVER THE FIRE...

...AND PUT IT OUT.

HISSS

?

WHAT'S THAT? IS IT THE FIRE? PERHAPS, THE WOOD WAS WET!

COME DOWN. IT'S NO USE CATCHING THE FLEDGLINGS TILL THE FIRE IS ABLAZE AGAIN.

HISSS

THE HUNTERS SOON HAD ANOTHER FIRE BLAZING.

THERE! NOW LET'S BRING THEM DOWN.

BUT AS SOON AS THEY WENT TO GET THE BIRDS, THE OSPREY ONCE AGAIN PUT OUT THE FIRE.

THIS WENT ON TILL MIDNIGHT. THE SHE-HAWK FELT SORRY FOR THE OSPREY.

HE'LL LOSE HIS LIFE TRYING TO SAVE OUR YOUNG ONES. GO TO FRIEND TORTOISE AND SEE IF HE CAN HELP.

WHEN THE HAWK FLEW TO THE TORTOISE AND TOLD HIM THE WHOLE STORY —

DON'T WORRY. I'LL COME THERE AS QUICKLY AS I CAN.

SOON —

HEY, LOOK! A HUGE TORTOISE! LET'S FORGET THE BIRDS AND CATCH HIM. WE'LL HAVE ENOUGH FOOD FOR DAYS.

THEY TORE THEIR WAISTBANDS INTO STRIPS...

...AND BOUND THE TORTOISE TO THEIR BODIES.

NOW, PULL AWAY!

I WILL! I WILL! I'LL PULL YOU ALL RIGHT!

SUDDENLY —

HEY!

HELP!

THAT SHOULD TAKE CARE OF YOU.

THE HUNTERS QUICKLY LOOSENED THE STRIPS OF CLOTH THAT BOUND THEM TO THE TORTOISE.

THE FELLOW IS DANGEROUS! LET'S LEAVE HIM HERE AND MAKE ANOTHER FIRE FOR OUR FLEDGLINGS.

THEY BEGAN TO COLLECT TWIGS.

THEY'RE BACK! GO TO THE LION AND SEEK HIS HELP.

GREED DOES NOT PAY

THERE ONCE WAS A BRAHMANA WHO HAD A WIFE AND THREE DAUGHTERS. HE LOVED THEM DEARLY AND TOOK GOOD CARE OF THEM.

THEN SUDDENLY ONE DAY HE DIED.

HOW COULD HE LEAVE US AND GO? WHO WILL CARE FOR US NOW?

SOME KIND NEIGHBOURS WHO HEARD HER WAILING RUSHED IN.

WE WILL. WE WON'T LET YOU STARVE. NOW PLEASE WIPE YOUR TEARS.

MEANWHILE, THE BRAHMANA WAS REBORN AS A GOLDEN SWAN. ONE DAY —

I MUST GO AND SEE HOW MY WIFE AND DAUGHTERS ARE GETTING ALONG.

HE FLEW TO HIS VILLAGE.

THEY LIVE ON CHARITY! HOW DEGRADING!! I MUST DO SOMETHING TO HELP THEM.

BUT WHAT CAN I... HEY! I'VE GOT IT!

A LITTLE LATER —

MOTHER! LOOK! A GOLDEN BIRD! LET'S CATCH IT!

WAIT! I AM YOUR HUSBAND, REBORN AS A BIRD.

I CAN'T BEAR TO SEE YOUR PLIGHT. I'LL GIVE YOU ONE OF MY FEATHERS. SELL IT AND USE THE MONEY TO BUY FOOD AND CLOTHING.

HE PLUCKED OUT ONE OF HIS GOLDEN FEATHERS...

...GAVE IT TO HER...

...AND FLEW AWAY.

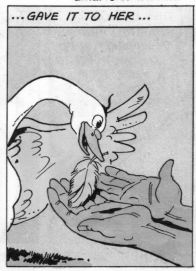

WEEK AFTER WEEK HE RETURNED TO GIVE HER YET ANOTHER FEATHER AND THE WIDOW SOON BECAME RICH.

BUT, ALAS! LIKE MOST RICH PEOPLE SHE BECAME GREEDY. ONE DAY—

SUPPOSE HE STOPS COMING? A MERE BIRD IS NOT TO BE TRUSTED.

THE NEXT TIME HE COMES, I'LL PLUCK OUT ALL HIS FEATHERS.

NO, MOTHER! YOU CAN'T DO THAT!

YOU CAN'T MEAN IT, MOTHER!

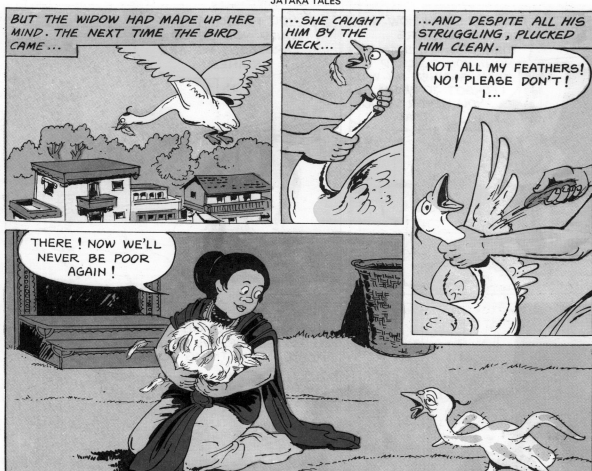

I'LL TELL YOU HOW. MY GOLDEN FEATHERS TURNED WHITE BECAUSE YOU...YOU PLUCKED THEM AGAINST MY WILL. I FORGOT TO WARN YOU NEVER TO DO THAT.

YOU FORGOT? HOW COULD YOU BE SO CARELESS! WE ARE RUINED!

THAT'S WHERE A USELESS BIRD BELONGS... THE DUSTBIN. ONE OF YOU GIVE HIM SOMETHING TO EAT.

WITHIN MONTHS, THE SWAN'S FEATHERS GREW AGAIN. BUT THEY WERE ALL WHITE.

WHAT'S THE USE OF STAYING ON HERE? I'D BETTER GO AWAY.

AS FOR THE GREEDY WIFE SHE SOON FINISHED ALL HER MONEY AND FELL UPON BAD DAYS AS SHE WELL DESERVED.

THE LOYAL GENERAL

LONG AGO IN VARANASI, THERE LIVED A KING CROW WHO HAD A MATE HE LOVED DEARLY.

ONE DAY, AS THEY FLEW PAST THE PALACE OF THE KING OF VARANASI, QUEEN CROW SAW A SIGHT WHICH MADE HER MOUTH WATER.

AH! HOW I WISH I COULD TASTE JUST A TINY BIT OF THAT FISH!

THE NEXT DAY —

COME, MY LOVE. LET'S GO OUT AND LOOK FOR SOME FOOD.

I DON'T WANT THE KIND OF FOOD WE FIND!

I WANT THE FOOD I SAW IN THE PALACE ON THE KING'S TABLE. IF I CAN'T HAVE IT, I'LL DIE.

AS THE KING CROW WONDERED WHAT HE SHOULD DO, HIS GENERAL CAME UP.

YOUR MAJESTY, WHAT'S THE MATTER?

WHEN THE KING CROW TOLD HIM —

OH! IS THAT ALL? DON'T WORRY. I'LL SEE THAT OUR QUEEN HAS THE FOOD SHE CRAVES FOR.

TAKING EIGHT OF THE BEST CROWS WITH HIM, THE GENERAL FLEW TOWARDS THE PALACE.

LET'S PERCH ON THE KITCHEN ROOF.

NOW LISTEN CAREFULLY. WHILE THE FOOD IS BEING TAKEN TO THE KING, I'LL MAKE THE COOK DROP THE DISHES.

FOUR OF YOU MUST THEN FILL YOUR BEAKS WITH RICE AND FOUR WITH FISH, AND FLY TO OUR QUEEN.

AH! HERE COMES THE COOK! WHEN HE REACHES THE OPEN COURTYARD, I'LL STRIKE!

THE NEXT MOMENT —

AIEEE!

AIEEEE!

DROP THOSE DISHES AND CATCH THAT WICKED CROW!

THE MOMENT THE DISHES WERE DROPPED, THE CHOSEN EIGHT FILLED THEIR BEAKS AND FLEW AWAY.

AH! THE QUEEN'S LONGING WILL BE SATISFIED. THEY CAN DO WHAT THEY WILL WITH ME, NOW!

GOOD! YOU'VE GOT HIM! BRING HIM HERE.

O, CROW! YOU HAVE DARED TO DISPLEASE ME. AND IN THIS FOOLISH VENTURE YOU'VE RISKED YOUR VERY LIFE! WHY DID YOU DO IT?

FOR MY KING. HE TOLD ME ABOUT THE QUEEN'S LONGING FOR THE FOOD SHE SAW ON YOUR TABLE. I PROMISED TO GET IT FOR HER — AND I HAVE KEPT MY PROMISE.

THE BIRD WAS WILLING TO SACRIFICE HIS LIFE FOR HIS KING! SUCH LOYALTY IS RARE! HE MUST BE REWARDED.

SET HIM FREE!

HENCEFORTH A PORTION OF THE FOOD COOKED FOR ME, SHALL BE SENT EVERY DAY TO YOU AND YOUR KING AND QUEEN. AND A LARGE MEASURE OF RICE SHALL BE COOKED FOR YOUR KING'S FOLLOWING.

PRACTISE WHAT YOU PREACH

ONCE THE KING OF THE BIRDS TOOK HIS FLOCK TO THE HIMALAYAS IN SEARCH OF FOOD.

NOW GO AND LOOK FOR SEEDS AND GRAIN. WHEN YOU FIND SOME, REPORT TO ME, SO WE CAN ALL SHARE IT.

AS THEY WANDERED OFF, ONE OF THE BIRDS CAME TO A ROAD ALONG WHICH WAGONS LOADED WITH GRAIN USED TO PASS.

LOOK AT ALL THAT GRAIN ON THE ROAD. WHAT A FEAST! I WON'T TELL THE KING ABOUT THIS FIND!

BUT WHAT IF ONE OF THE OTHERS SHOULD FLY THIS WAY AND SEE THE GRAIN?

I KNOW! I'LL TELL THEM ABOUT IT AND YET KEEP THEM AWAY!

SHE FLEW BACK.

YOU'VE BEEN AWAY A LONG TIME! HAVE YOU HAD ANY LUCK?

NONE AT ALL! IN FACT, I VERY NEARLY LOST MY LIFE!

THE BIRDS WERE ALL EARS.

I HAPPENED TO FLY OVER THE HIGHWAY! ELEPHANTS AND HORSES, AND WAGONS DRAWN BY FIERCE BULLOCKS GO ALONG THAT ROUTE.

WAGONS? THEN THERE MUST BE PLENTY OF GRAIN THERE! AND...

THERE IS. BUT ONCE YOU ALIGHT IT'S DIFFICULT TO SOAR UP AGAIN. DON'T GO THAT WAY. IT'S DANGEROUS.

AFTER HER WARNING, THE OTHER BIRDS WERE CAREFUL TO AVOID THE HIGHWAY.

THAT WAS CLEVER OF ME! I HAVE ALL THIS GRAIN TO MYSELF NOW.

SUDDENLY —

WHRRRR

WHAT'S THAT?
OH! A CART!

IT'S A LONG WAY OFF.
THERE'S ENOUGH TIME
TO PECK A FEW MORE
SEEDS.

WHRRR

WHAT SHE DIDN'T KNOW WAS THAT IT WAS AN EXPRESS CART.

WHRRRR

WHRRRR

SUDDENLY —

OH! NO!
IT'S ALMOST
UPON ME!

BUT BEFORE SHE COULD TAKE WING,
THE CART RAN OVER HER.

WHRRRR

THAT EVENING, WHEN ALL THE BIRDS CAME HOME TO ROOST, THEY FOUND HER MISSING.

GO AND LOOK FOR HER.

THE BIRDS FLEW IN ALL DIRECTIONS IN SEARCH OF THEIR LOST COMPANION.

LATER, A FEW BIRDS REPORTED TO THE KING —

SHE'S DEAD!

WE FOUND HER ON THE HIGHWAY.... A CART MUST HAVE RUN OVER HER.

THE KING FLEW TO THE SPOT AT ONCE.

WHAT A SAD FATE! SHE WARNED YOU NOT TO GO NEAR THE HIGHWAY. BUT SHE COULD NOT CONTROL HER OWN GREED. LET THIS BE A LESSON TO ALL OF YOU!

THE GREEDY CROW

A PIGEON ONCE MADE ITS HOME IN THE KITCHEN OF A RICH MERCHANT OF VARANASI.

ONE DAY, A GREEDY CROW FLEW PAST.

MM-M! FISH! I MUST FIND MY WAY INTO THIS KITCHEN AND MAKE IT MY HOME. BUT HOW SHOULD I GO ABOUT IT?

JUST THEN HIS EYE FELL ON THE PIGEON.

I'VE GOT IT! I'LL MAKE FRIENDS WITH HIM!

AS THE PIGEON FLEW OUT IN SEARCH OF FOOD, THE CROW FOLLOWED HIM. AFTER A WHILE —

WHY DO YOU FOLLOW ME, FRIEND?

I LIKE YOU. I WOULD LIKE TO FEED WITH YOU.

BUT WE DO NOT EAT THE SAME FOOD.

THAT DOESN'T MATTER. WHILE YOU PECK GRASS SEEDS, I'LL LOOK FOR WORMS.

ALL RIGHT. FOLLOW ME THEN, BUT DON'T DISTURB ME.

I'VE WON THE FIRST ROUND!

TOWARDS EVENING, AS THE PIGEON FLEW BACK INTO THE KITCHEN, THE CROW FOLLOWED HIM IN.

WHY! OUR PIGEON HAS BROUGHT A FRIEND! I MUST HANG UP ANOTHER BASKET FOR HIM.

SECOND ROUND WON!

24

AND SO THE CROW, TOO, BEGAN TO LIVE IN THE KITCHEN. THEN, ONE EVENING AS THE TWO RETURNED HOME —

THE MASTER IS HAVING A BANQUET TOMORROW. CLEAN AND CUT ALL THIS FISH TONIGHT.

LOOK AT HIS MOUTH WATER!

WHAT LUCK! I'VE ALREADY EATEN MY FILL TODAY. TOMORROW I'LL FEAST — NOT ON WORMS BUT ON FISH!

THAT NIGHT —

AA-A-AH! OO-OH!

WHAT'S THE MATTER WITH YOU?

I DON'T KNOW! IT MUST BE THE WORMS I ATE TODAY!

OR IS IT THE FISH YOU WANT TO EAT TOMORROW?

THE NEXT MORNING —

COME ON, LET'S GO.

I'M NOT COMING TODAY. YOU GO ALONE. I HAVE A TERRIBLE STOMACHACHE.

NONSENSE! IT'S THE FISH, ISN'T IT? TAKE MY ADVICE. IT IS DANGEROUS TO TOUCH MEN'S FOOD. COME, LET'S GO. UP WITH YOU!

WHAT! AND GIVE UP WHAT I CAME HERE FOR IN THE FIRST PLACE! NEVER!

I DO HAVE A STOMACHACHE. YOU GO.

ALL RIGHT, I'M GOING. BUT TAKE CARE.

AS THE PIGEON FLEW OUT, THE COOK ENTERED AND SET TO WORK.

THESE PIECES I'LL FRY. AND THESE I'LL PUT INTO THE CURRY.

AH! THE BEST BITS ARE TO BE FRIED! I'LL SETTLE FOR FRIED FISH!

WHEN THE FOOD WAS READY, THE COOK COVERED THE DISHES.

I'LL GO OUT AND REST FOR A WHILE TILL THE MAID COMES FOR THE FOOD.

IT IS HIGH TIME YOU WENT OUT. I CANNOT WAIT ANY LONGER.

AS SOON AS THE COOK'S BACK WAS TURNED —

I'LL TAKE A LARGE PIECE OF FRIED FISH AND FLY BACK TO MY BASKET.

I CAN EAT IT THERE IN PEACE WITHOUT BEING FOUND OUT.

SUDDENLY —

OH! OH! WHAT HAVE I DONE!

CLANNG
CLANGGG

THE COOK TURNED ROUND —

WHAT WAS THAT?

BEFORE THE STARTLED CROW COULD REALISE WHAT WAS HAPPENING, THE COOK POUNCED ON HIM.

I'LL PLUCK YOU CLEAN AND SOAK YOU IN A MIXTURE OF SOUR BUTTERMILK AND SPICES!

LATER —

O-O-OH! A-A-AH!

THAT SHOULD TEACH YOU NEVER TO BE GREEDY AGAIN!

THAT EVENING WHEN THE PIGEON FLEW IN AND SAW THE CROW'S PLIGHT —

ALAS, MY GREEDY FRIEND IF ONLY YOU HAD LISTENED TO ME!

THE BULBUL AND THE HORNBILL

THE HORNBILL WAS ONCE THE KING OF THE BIRDS. BUT HE USED TO KILL SMALLER BIRDS IF THEY MADE THE SLIGHTEST MISTAKE.

SO ONE DAY ALL THE BIRDS GOT TOGETHER AND DECIDED THAT THEY MUST HAVE A NEW KING. THEIR CHOICE FELL ON THE BULBUL.

HE HAS A REGAL APPEARANCE...

...AND HE COULD NOT HURT ANYONE EVEN IF HE WANTED TO.

BUT HOW DO WE BREAK THE NEWS TO THE HORNBILL? HE WON'T BE PLEASED.

I HAVE AN IDEA.

I'LL NEED YOUR HELP, WOODPECKER. COME WITH ME.

SOMETIME LATER —

O KING, WE FEEL THAT YOU SHOULD UNDERGO A TEST AND PROVE YOUR WORTH. YOU WILL HAVE TO SIT ON A THICK BRANCH AND BREAK IT.

IF YOU DON'T SUCCEED, WHOEVER DOES SHALL BE DEEMED WORTHIER OF RULING US.

TELL ME WHICH BRANCH I SHOULD SIT ON.

THAT'S THE BRANCH.

IF I CANNOT BREAK THE BRANCH WHO CAN?

THE HORNBILL FLEW UP TO IT...

...AND LANDED ON IT WITH ALL HIS MIGHT.

BUT THE BRANCH DID NOT BREAK.

REMEMBER, ANYONE WHO ENTERS THE CONTEST MUST SIT ON AN EQUALLY THICK BRANCH.

THE BULBUL IS THE NEXT CONTESTANT. IS THE BRANCH OVER THERE THICK ENOUGH?

THAT BRANCH IS EVEN THICKER THAN THIS.

IF THE BULBUL CAN BREAK THAT BRANCH HE CERTAINLY DESERVES TO BE KING.

GO ON!

WHAT THE HORNBILL DIDN'T KNOW WAS THAT THE BRANCH ON WHICH THE BULBUL WAS TO SIT HAD BEEN BORED THROUGH BY THE WOODPECKER.

AND WHEN THE BULBUL LANDED ON IT —

CRACK

HE...HE HAS BROKEN THE BRANCH.

THE HORNBILL ACKNOWLEDGING DEFEAT FLEW AWAY.

AND THE BULBUL BECAME KING OF THE BIRDS.

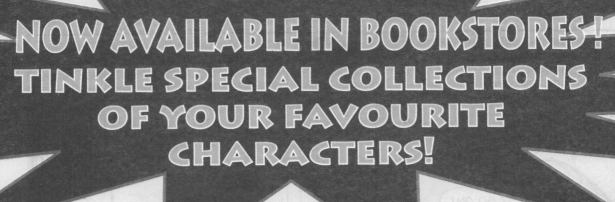